Disney

# THE STOLEN EGG

By Sue Vyner

Illustrated by
Tim Vyner

Viking

Something was coming . . .

With a great flapping of her dark wings,
the albatross swooped down upon the egg.

Did she think it was her own egg, stolen from her nest
while she was off searching for food?

She took up the egg in her beak and flew across the land,
over the seas, to a place far away.

Where before the land was cold and snowy and barren, now
it was warm and fertile, with a hot sun shining overhead.

Gently the albatross placed the egg in the grass.

But something was coming . . .

. . . hissing as it slithered near and frightening the albatross away.

Coming upon the egg, the snake picked it up and
carried it in her mouth as she glided through the grass,
into the forest, to her nest in the hole.

But the shell of the egg was too hard—
not like the softer shells of her own babies' eggs.
So she took the egg and put it down at the edge of the swamp.

But something was coming . . .

. . . swirling through the muddy waters of the swamp.
Hissing, the snake slithered away, back to her hole in the forest.

The crocodile picked up the egg between her
sharp teeth and carried it away from the forest,
into the swamp, to her nest on the mound.

But the egg was too round, not like the oval
shape of her own babies' eggs.

So she took the egg and put it down in the sand.

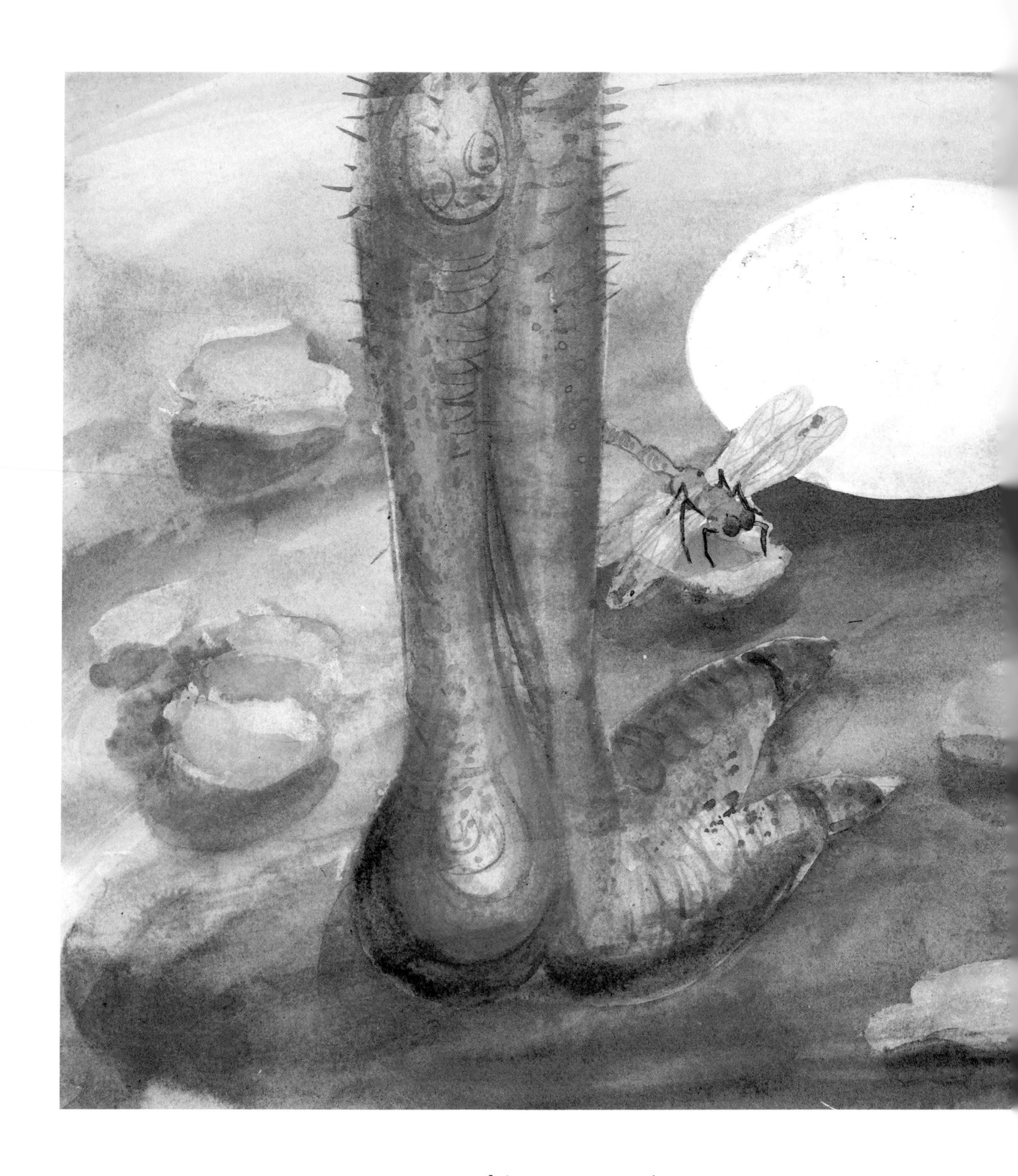

But something was coming . . .

. . . running closer with loud thumping sounds.

With a squawk, the ostrich picked up the egg with her beak and tucked it under her wing. Then she ran out of the sand, over the plain, to her nest on the ground.

But the egg was much smaller than her own babies' eggs.

So she took the egg and put it down among the dunes.

But something was coming . . .

. . . moving slowly and steadily across the sand.

The tortoise pushed the egg over the ground,
across the dunes, to her nest in the sand.

But it was much bigger than her own babies' eggs.

So she rolled the egg toward the beach.

But something was coming, flying toward the
egg where it lay quietly on the shore.

It was the albatross again!

With a loud shriek, she swooped down
and picked up the egg in her beak.

She flew tirelessly across the land, over the seas . . .

. . . back to the cold, barren place far
away where she had first found the egg.

And gently she placed
it back in the snow.

But something was coming, shuffling
close on black webbed feet.

With a cry, the penguin bent down, pushed the egg
onto his feet, and shuffled away from the cliffs,
through the snow, and back to his place on the ice.

Then he settled down to wait, keeping the egg
safe and warm on his feet, until . . .

Something was coming, this time from inside the egg!

## WANDERING ALBATROSS

The wandering albatross is the largest flying bird, with a wingspan of over 9 feet. It lives for about 30 years and every year it flies huge distances over the southern oceans, always returning to the same nesting ground and the same mate. Each year the female lays only 1 egg.

## GABOON VIPER

The Gaboon viper is the largest viper in the world, the female growing to be about 6 feet long, twice the length of the male. It's so poisonous its venom could kill 20 people. This viper has the longest fangs of any snake, about the length of an adult's thumb. It lives around 10 years in the tropical rain forests of Africa. Most species of snake lay eggs, but some, such as the Gaboon viper, give birth to live young. The baby snakes develop in egg sacs, hatching inside the mother, and are born live. However, in certain conditions the young may emerge from the mother's body still in their egg sacs and hatch shortly afterwards.

## NILE CROCODILE

Crocodiles are reptiles that inhabited the earth at the time of the dinosaurs. The Nile crocodile lives for between 25 and 50 years and may grow to as long as 16 feet. It lives in the rivers and swamps of tropical Africa where the female lays between 50 and 80 eggs. When they hatch she carries them in her mouth to the edge of the water.

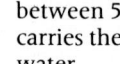

## AFRICAN SPURRED TORTOISE

The African spurred tortoise grows to almost 3 feet in length—about the size of a large dog—and lives in the dry regions of Africa. These reptiles are well known for their long lifespans, some living for over one hundred years. The female lays a clutch of up to 17 eggs.

## AFRICAN OSTRICH

The African ostrich is the largest flightless bird, often over 6 feet tall. It's the swiftest living creature on 2 legs, running faster than the fastest human sprinter. It lives for about 40 years on the dry plains of Africa. The female lays about 12 eggs which are the largest of any living animal. They are so strong that they can bear the weight of a very heavy man.

## EMPEROR PENGUIN

The Emperor penguin is the largest of all marine birds, standing about 3 feet tall, and although it can't fly, it's an excellent swimmer. This penguin lives in the Antarctic, which is the coldest place in the world. Each year the female lays 1 egg, straight onto the ice, and the male keeps it warm in a flap on his feet until the chick is hatched. Thousands of males huddle together in this way, in temperatures far colder than the inside of a fridge.

Note: The eggs on these two pages do not represent their actual size relative to their parent. They are meant to show the varying and relative sizes and shapes of the eggs that are featured in this book.

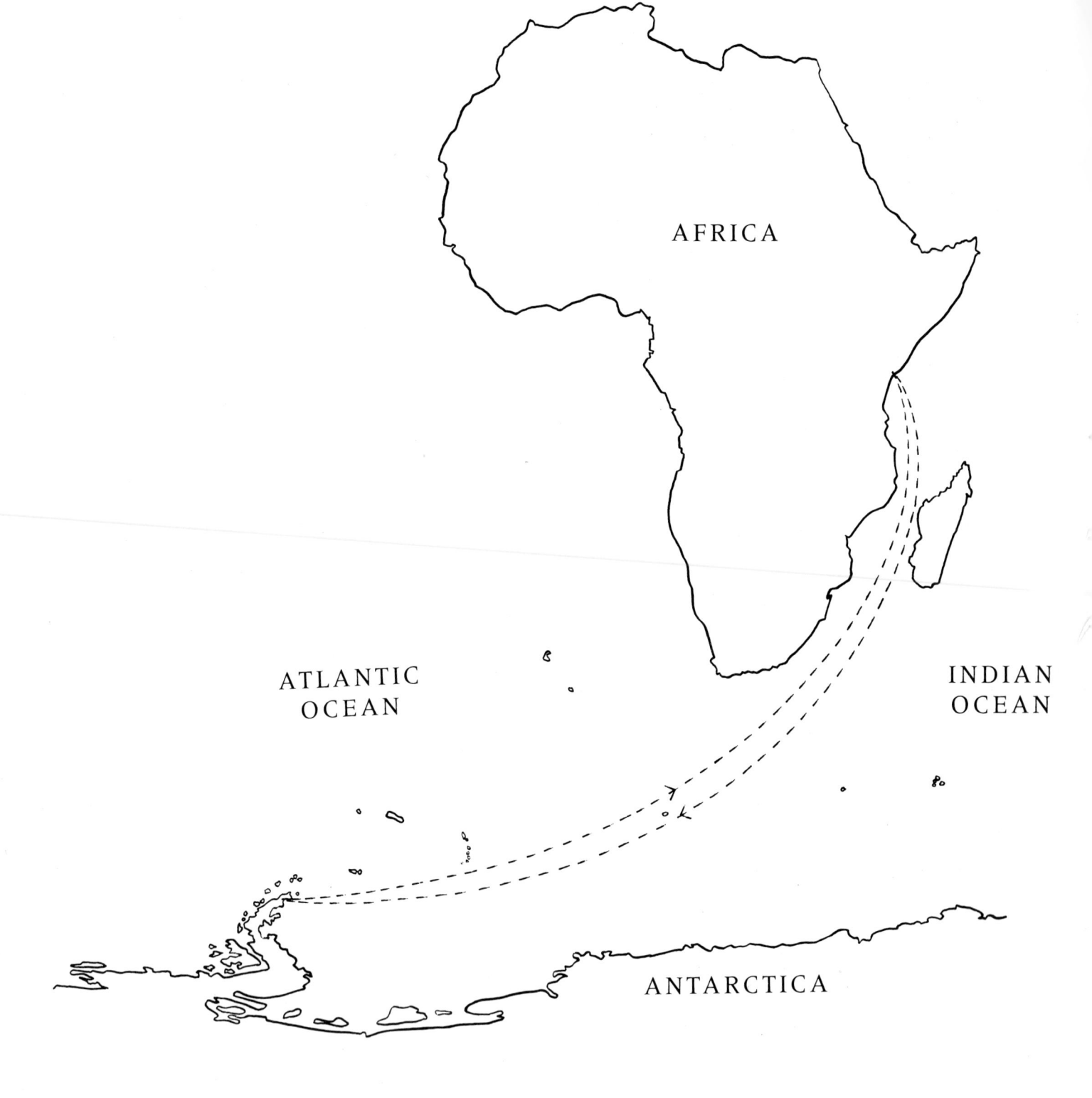

**VIKING**
Published by the Penguin Group
Viking Penguin, a division of Penguin Books USA Inc.,
375 Hudson Street, New York, New York 10014, U.S.A.

First published in Great Britain by Victor Gollancz Ltd. 1991
First American edition published in 1992

1  3  5  7  9  10  8  6  4  2

Library of Congress Card Catalog Number: 91-50623
ISBN 0−670−84460−8
Printed in Singapore by Imago Publishing Ltd